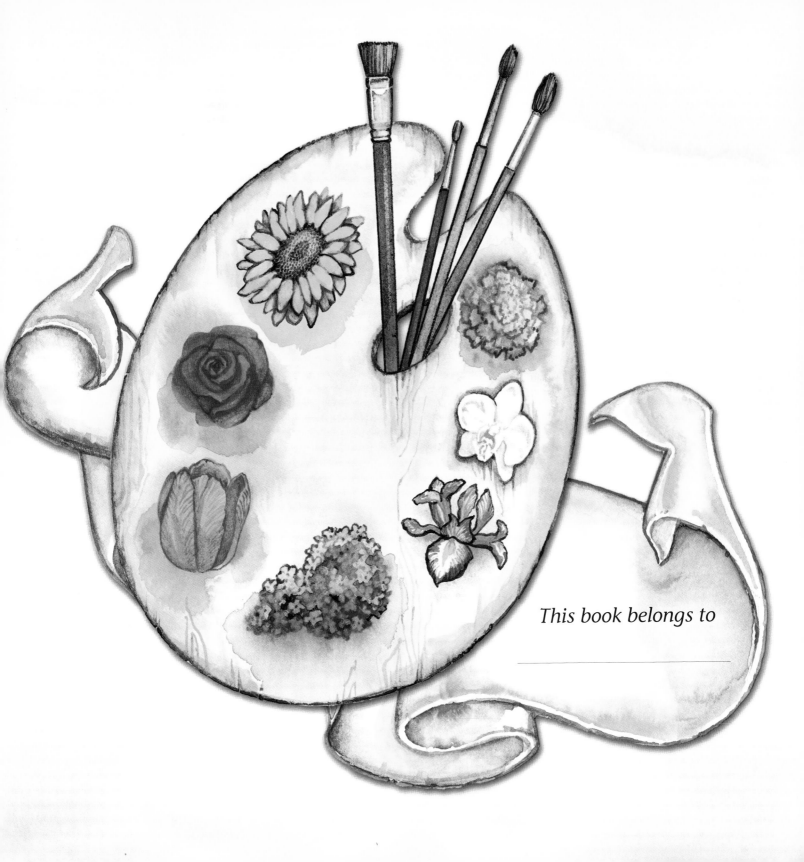

This book belongs to

_____

# Natalia's Favorite Color

WRITTEN BY

Rosanna Eubank Dude

ILLUSTRATED BY

Patricia Reeder Eubank

ideals children's books.
Nashville, Tennessee

ISBN-13: 978-0-8249-5523-6

Published by Ideals Children's Books
An imprint of Ideals Publications
A Guideposts Company
535 Metroplex Drive, Suite 250
Nashville, Tennessee 37211
www.idealsbooks.com

Color separations by Precision Color Graphics, Franklin, Wisconsin
Printed and bound in Italy

Library of Congress CIP data on file

Designed by Georgina Rucker

10 9 8 7 6 5 4 3 2 1

*For both of my grandmothers, two amazing and beautiful*
*women full of elegance, strength, and creativity.*
—R. E. D.

*For the same two wonderful grandmothers,*
*who have given so much.*
—P. R. E.

atalia hopped out of bed and put on her purple
dress. She pulled on her striped tights and her pink
boots. She grabbed her patchwork coat and ran downstairs.

Today was Natalia's favorite day of the week.

Today was Wednesday, art class day.

or Natalia, the morning seemed to go so slowly! But finally, it was time for art. Ms. Rohde handed out sheets of paper covered with different colors.

"Let's choose our favorite color," Ms. Rohde said.

"Orange!" called Ramon.

"Blue," said Danny.

"Purple," said Monique.

"What is your favorite, Natalia?" asked Ms. Rohde.

Natalia just looked down at her paper. She couldn't choose a favorite.

"That's okay," said Ms. Rohde. "Think about it, and tell us next week.

But Natalia wasn't sure she could choose by next week.

hat afternoon, Natalia went to her grandmother's flower shop. She told her about art class. "I don't have a favorite color!" Natalia said sadly.

Grandmother laughed and kissed her forehead. "If you help me with my project, I think you will know your favorite color by next week's art class."

rom one of the giant tin pails that held fresh flowers, Grandmother chose a bundle of pale pink flowers.

"These are carnations, Natalia," she said. "Many hundreds of years ago, monks in Italy began to cultivate these little flowers.

Grandmother placed the pink carnations into a large pot.

When Natalia's mom picked her up, she whispered in Grandmother's ear, "I think my favorite color is pink."

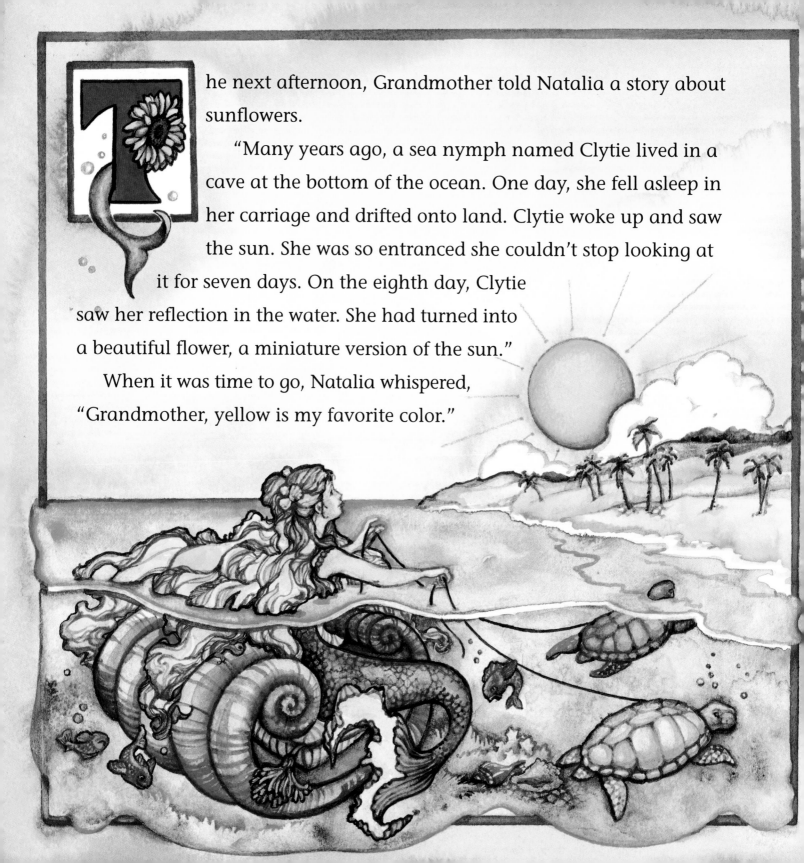

he next afternoon, Grandmother told Natalia a story about sunflowers.

"Many years ago, a sea nymph named Clytie lived in a cave at the bottom of the ocean. One day, she fell asleep in her carriage and drifted onto land. Clytie woke up and saw the sun. She was so entranced she couldn't stop looking at it for seven days. On the eighth day, Clytie saw her reflection in the water. She had turned into a beautiful flower, a miniature version of the sun."

When it was time to go, Natalia whispered, "Grandmother, yellow is my favorite color."

The next afternoon, Natalia ran into the flower shop and saw bright blue flowers. Grandmother said, "Natalia, these beautiful flowers are irises. The Dutch artist Vincent van Gogh painted irises because of their bold color and unusual shape.

Natalia thought the iris bouquet was lovely.

When she left, she whispered, "Grandmother, I think blue is my favorite color."

n Saturday, Natalia worked all day in her grandmother's shop. After lunch, Grandmother said, "Natalia, let's make a bouquet of lilacs. Both George Washington and Thomas Jefferson had lilac bushes in their gardens."

Natalia and Grandmother bundled the purple flowers together and tied a great big bow of purple velvet around them.

When it was time to go home, Natalia hugged her grandmother and whispered, "Purple, definitely purple, is my favorite color."

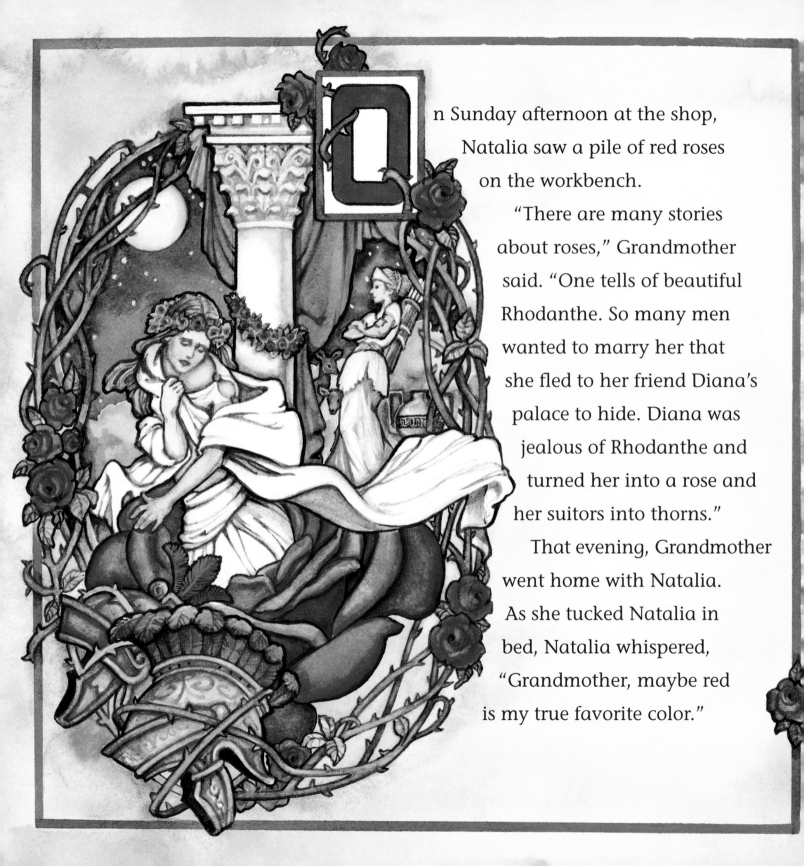

On Sunday afternoon at the shop, Natalia saw a pile of red roses on the workbench.

"There are many stories about roses," Grandmother said. "One tells of beautiful Rhodanthe. So many men wanted to marry her that she fled to her friend Diana's palace to hide. Diana was jealous of Rhodanthe and turned her into a rose and her suitors into thorns."

That evening, Grandmother went home with Natalia. As she tucked Natalia in bed, Natalia whispered, "Grandmother, maybe red is my true favorite color."

n Monday afternoon, Natalia skipped into her grandmother's shop. Grandmother said to Natalia, "Today you will see the beauty of simplicity. These white flowers are orchids. Many years ago, the Chinese called orchids 'the plant of the King's Fragrance'."

Natalia climbed off her stool to select some orchids, but Grandmother said, "Just one, Natalia."

Natalia took a long time choosing the most beautiful orchid. She carefully brought it back to the counter.

Grandmother placed the orchid into a glass vase with rocks and water. "It's beautiful!" cried Natalia.

As Natalia was leaving her grandmother's shop, she ran back. "Grandmother, is it okay if white is my favorite color?"

Her grandmother just smiled, "Of course, dear."

蘭花

The next afternoon, Natalia's grandmother was surrounded by flowers of every color imaginable.

"Aren't these tulips magnificent?" Grandmother said. "The word tulip comes from the Turkish word for turban. Doesn't the flower resemble the shape of a turban? Shall we make a bouquet from these brightly colored tulips?"

Natalia and Grandmother gathered armfuls of deep orange tulips and carried them to the table.

"What should we put them in, dear?" Grandmother asked.

Natalia chose a round vase. "Grandmother," she said. "I love orange. It might even be my favorite color."

Natalia and Grandmother placed the tulips into the vase, making a splash of orange that glowed in the sunlight.

As Natalia gathered her coat to leave, Grandmother asked if she was eager for art class tomorrow. Natalia frowned and looked down at her shoes.

"No, Grandmother. Ms. Rohde will ask me again, in front of everybody, to tell my favorite color. I don't have a favorite color."

Grandmother smiled and gave Natalia a big hug. "Don't worry, Natalia. You will know just what to say to Ms. Rohde."

**T**he next morning, as Natalia slowly ate her cereal, the doorbell rang. Natalia ran to open the door. On the doorstep was a huge bouquet. Natalia gasped. It was the most beautiful thing she had ever seen!

er mom read the card that came with the flowers.

*My Dear Natalia,*
*Why should you have to choose only*
*one color to love? All colors are wonderful!*
*Love,*
*Grandmother*

Grandmother was right. Natalia couldn't choose just *one* favorite color. She loved all colors!

Her mom laughed and kissed Natalia's head. "It's true" she said. "Artists don't love just one color. They love them all!"

**N**atalia headed to school, and art class, knowing that she was an artist. And she would tell Ms. Rohde and the whole class that she loved all colors!

The End

TULIPS

ROSES

"GYPSOPHILA"
PARROT

"MAGNOLIA"
NEWFOUNDLAND
DOG

"GARDENIA"
RAGDOLL
CAT

CARNATIONS

ORCHIDS

SUNFLOWERS

IRISES

LILACS

*Natalia's Flower Palette of Color*